This igloo book belongs to:

••

igloobooks

Published in 2013
by Igloo Books Ltd
Cottage Farm
Sywell
NN6 0BJ
www.igloobooks.com

SHE001 0713
2 4 6 8 10 9 7 5 3
ISBN: 978-0-85780-776-2

Printed and manufactured in China

Illustrated by:
Alice Bonacina, Boaz Gabai, Caroline Romanet, Diane Le Feyer, Gerald Kelly,
Mays Dabs, Mike Love, Stefano Tambellini

Written by:
Jenny Woods, Joff Brown, Jan Payne

The Brothers Grimm
Treasured Fairytales

igloobooks

Contents

Contents

Sleeping Beauty

Once, long ago, there was a king and queen who wanted a child more than anything. They waited for many years, but finally, their wish came true. On a fine summer day, their beautiful, baby daughter was born. The king and queen were overjoyed.

"We shall have a fantastic feast!" cried the king. Everyone at the palace was busy making preparations for a magnificent party to celebrate the arrival of the new princess.

Friends and family were invited to the celebration. The king also asked the fairies who lived in his kingdom, all except one, who was very grumpy.

On the day of the party there was music and dancing and a splendid feast. Guests brought lovely presents for the baby. The gifts from the fairies were the most wonderful of all.

The first fairy gave the princess the gift of beauty and the second granted her the gift of kindness. The third fairy approached the princess's crib, but before she could speak, the sky turned dark and a crack of thunder boomed through the palace.

Another fairy suddenly appeared. She was furious that she had not been invited to the party.

"My gift to the princess is a curse," she shrieked. "On her sixteenth birthday she will prick her finger on a spinning wheel and die!" With a swirl of smoke and a crackle of magic she was gone.

The guests were shocked into silence but the third fairy thought fast.

"I can't undo her curse but I can lessen it," she said. "The princess will not die, instead she will fall asleep for one hundred years."

The king ordered every spinning wheel in the land to be burned. No one told the princess about the curse and she grew up happy and carefree.

On her sixteenth birthday, she was so excited she got up early and went in search of her presents. The princess was sure her parents had bought her something special, they had been acting so strangely for the last few days.

She searched room after room but found nothing new until she came across a small door. She turned the rusty key and stepped inside.

In the middle of the room sat an old woman at a spinning wheel. It was the angry fairy. She had come to make sure her curse came true.

The princess had never seen a spinning wheel before and watched in wonder as it turned wool into thread.

"Would you like to have a go?" asked the old woman.

"Yes, please," said the princess, who had been given the gift of good manners. The princess sat down and began to spin.

"Ouch!" the princess cried as she pricked her finger. Suddenly, she felt very tired and spotted a bed in the corner of the room. The princess stumbled on to the bed and fell asleep.

At the very same moment everyone in the palace fell into a deep slumber. The cook lay her head on the birthday cake she had been icing and started to snore.

The king and queen, who were still in bed, turned over and dropped back off to sleep. Even the royal cat and dog curled up in their baskets to snooze.

Everything was silent and still. As the days and weeks went by, thick brambles grew up outside and the palace was almost hidden from view.

The story of the sleeping princess spread across the land. Many brave men came to rescue her, but they could not cut through the thick, thorny branches.

Then one day, a prince came riding through the woods. He too had heard the tale of the beautiful princess who slept in an enchanted palace. When he saw the royal flag fluttering above a tangle of wild bushes, he knew he had found the right place.

Determined to rescue her from the evil curse, the prince swung his sword through the brambles.

Ignoring the scratches from the spiky thorns, the prince carried on until he had cut a path to the palace door. He stepped over the sleeping guards and went inside.

The prince rushed from room to room, past slumbering servants and dozing pets. At last he reached the room where the princess lay.

As soon as the prince saw sleeping beauty, he fell in love. The princess was so beautiful. The prince gave her a kiss and with the lightest touch of his lips, the curse was broken.

The princess awoke and her heart filled with love when she saw the handsome prince. He took her hand and together they walked through the palace where everyone was stretching and yawning as they woke up from their long slumber.

The king and queen were delighted that the curse had been broken. They arranged a magnificent wedding for the prince and princess with music, dancing and a splendid feast. Everyone had a wonderful time and they all lived happily ever after, except the grumpy fairy who was never seen ever again.

12 Dancing Princesses

Once upon a time, there was a king who had twelve daughters. The princesses slept in twelve beds in one room. Every night they would go to bed, but in the morning their shoes were worn out, as if they had been dancing all night.

The king locked their bedroom door and even stationed guards outside, but it was no use. Every morning, the princesses' dancing shoes were worn out.

The king became more and more troubled about his daughters. They hardly spoke to him and they always seemed dreamy. Whenever the king asked why, they just laughed.

Eventually, the king decided that something had to be done.

"Whoever finds out the secret of my daughters' worn-out shoes can have half my fortune," proclaimed the king. "He can also marry whichever princess he likes, too!"

Many brave princes and knights arrived at the castle. They all swore they would find out the princesses' secret, but as each one stood guard, the princesses gave him a goblet of wine. The wine was enchanted and made the princes and knights fall into a deep sleep.

When they woke in the morning, the princesses' shoes were as worn out as ever and the men went home empty handed.

One day, a soldier arrived at the castle. "I have a magic cloak that makes the wearer invisible," he told the king. "Maybe it will help me solve this mystery."

The king agreed and the soldier went to guard the princesses. When they were about to go to bed, the eldest princess handed the soldier a glass of wine. When the princesses weren't looking, the soldier quickly poured the wine into a nearby jug.

Then the soldier laid down and pretended to go to sleep. After a while, he heard the princesses getting up from their beds. They all giggled as they put on their finest clothes.

"Our enchanted wine has sent that silly soldier to sleep," said the eldest princess.

"Are you sure he's really sleeping?" said the youngest princess.

The soldier pretended to snore very loudly.

"Of course he is," said the eldest princess. She clapped her hands three times and a little trapdoor flew open.

All the princesses rushed through the trapdoor. Quickly, the soldier put on his cloak and became invisible. He ran past the princesses, down the secret stairway.

"What was that?" said the youngest princess. "Someone went past!"

"It was just a cold breeze," said the eldest princess.

The soldier followed the princesses down a long, dark tunnel that led far underground. The tunnel led to a forest full of silver trees. The princesses ran on through a forest of gold, and then another forest where all the trees were made of diamonds.

Soon the princesses reached the shores of a great underground lake. In twelve little boats, twelve handsome princes were waiting.

The princesses each boarded a boat and the soldier followed. Invisible in his cloak, he climbed into the boat with the eldest princess and her handsome prince. The boats headed for a faraway island.

"How strange," said the prince to the eldest princess. "I must be tired today. My arms ache and I'm rowing much slower than usual."

The soldier stayed as quiet as he could until they reached the island. The princesses climbed out of the boats and went to a dazzling palace.

The princes and the princesses danced all night long. None of them could see the soldier, so he had to keep jumping out of their way in case they bumped into him and revealed his secret.

After many hours, the princesses had danced so much that their dancing shoes were worn and tattered.

The princes rowed the princesses back to the forest, and this time the soldier sat in the boat with the eldest princess.

"The king will never believe this!" thought the soldier. "I must bring him proof."

So as they went back through the forests of diamond, gold and silver, the soldier broke a twig from the trees. With each loud snap, the youngest princess jumped.

"Someone's following us!" she said. But the eldest princess always ignored her warnings.

As the princesses reached the trapdoor, the soldier crept past them and ran up the stairs. He took the cloak off, lay down and started snoring loudly. The princesses thought he had been asleep all the time and got into bed just before dawn.

The next morning, the soldier took the twigs of silver, gold and diamond straight to the king.

"I have solved the mystery, your majesty!" he said.

The king called the princesses to him and the soldier told his story. When he'd finished, something magical happened. The twelve princesses rubbed their eyes, blinked and looked around them, as if they had just woken up.

"We were enchanted!" they said. "Those twelve magical princes had cast a spell on us and made us dance every night!"

"Thank you for freeing us from the spell!" said the youngest princess.

The king gave the soldier half of his fortune. He fell in love and married the youngest princess and they danced every night.

The Elves and the Shoemaker

Long ago, there lived a shoemaker and his wife who were very poor. They only had enough money to buy leather for one last pair of shoes.

"I must make and sell these shoes tomorrow," said the shoemaker sadly. "Otherwise there will be no money for food." Wearily, he put the leather in his workshop and went to bed.

The next morning when the shoemaker came downstairs, he found that the leather had been made into a pair of beautiful shoes.

"Who could have done such amazing work?" asked the shoemaker. He put the shoes in the window and soon sold them. With the money, the shoemaker was able to buy leather for two pairs of shoes.

That night, the shoemaker left the leather out on his old workbench.

The next morning, when he came downstairs, he saw two pairs of shoes. They were so finely made, they sold instantly.

"Now I have enough money to buy leather for four pairs of shoes," said the happy shoemaker. That night, as before, he left the leather in his workshop.

Sure enough, the next morning, there were four pairs of beautiful shoes waiting on the workbench. The delighted shoemaker was able to buy more and more leather and each day he found more and more perfectly made shoes.

Soon, the shoemaker's little shoe shop became famous throughout the land. The shoemaker and his wife became rich, but they still had no idea who was making the shoes.

"We must find out," said the shoemaker's wife.

So, that night, they hid behind a curtain in the workshop and waited. The sun went down and soon it grew dark. The shoemaker and his wife watched and waited, but nothing happened.

Then, at midnight, the shoemaker and his wife heard scampering and chattering. They peeped around the curtain and saw two tiny elves dressed in rags. The elves climbed up onto the workbench and picked up the leather. Astonished, the shoemaker and his wife watched in wonder as the elves set to work.

Very carefully, one cut the leather with scissors. The other picked up a needle and a spool of silk thread and began to sew. The two elves worked so fast, their hands hardly seemed to move. They snipped and sewed and hammered, until suddenly there was a beautiful pair of shoes on the workbench.

The elves worked on into the night and after many hours they had turned all the leather into shoes. When they had finished, just before the sun rose, they dashed out of the door.

No matter how much leather the old shoemaker bought, the elves would arrive each night and make even more shoes.

The shoemaker continued to make lots of money, but there was something troubling him.

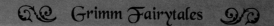

"Even though we have grown rich from the work of the elves, I still miss making shoes myself," he said to his wife. "The elves have brought us so much happiness. I wish we could do something to repay them."

Then the shoemaker had an idea.

"Their clothes are so ragged and worn. I think it's time we did something for them."

With the money they had made, the shoemaker and his wife bought the finest material they could find.

His wife cut and sewed until she had made two tiny suits of the richest crimson and gold, as well as two tiny hats to go with them.

The shoemaker made two tiny pairs of shoes in the softest leather. When they were finished, the clothes and shoes were laid out on the workbench.

"We must see if they like their presents!" said the shoemaker's wife. So, she and the shoemaker hid behind the curtain again. They waited until they heard the door creaking open and the elves scampered in.

When the elves saw the tiny suits, they jumped for joy. They threw off their ragged old clothes and tried on their new ones. They looked very smart indeed! When they saw the tiny shoes, they leapt up and down in excitement.

"Nobody has ever made us shoes before!" they cried.

When they were all dressed up, the elves admired each other.

"Now we're much too smart to make shoes any more!" they said.

With that, the two little elves jumped off the workbench and ran out of the door.

The shoemaker and his wife were sorry to see the elves go, but then the shoemaker looked at all the leather they had left behind.

"At last," he said, "I can make my own shoes again!"

The shoemaker set to work straight away. He spent all day hammering and sewing, making shoes that were even more beautiful than before.

The shoemaker and his wife were very happy. People came from miles away to buy his wonderful shoes and they were never poor again. The elves never returned to the little shop, but the shoemaker and his wife never forgot them. They were always grateful to the tiny shoemakers, who had helped change their lives.

Snow White

Once upon a time, a king had a lovely baby daughter. She had hair as black as ebony, skin as white as snow and lips as red as cherries. Her name was Snow White.

Snow White's mother had died and the king wanted a new wife. He married a very beautiful, but jealous queen who had a magic mirror. Every day, the queen asked, "Mirror, mirror, on the wall, who is the fairest of us all?"

The mirror always answered, "Oh, beautiful queen, you are the fairest one of all."

Time passed and Snow White grew to be a beautiful young woman One morning, the queen looked into the mirror and asked,

"Mirror, mirror, on the wall, who is the fairest of us all?"

The mirror answered, "Snow White is the fairest one of all!"

The queen was furious. "I will not allow it!" she screamed. "I will get rid of Snow White." So, the wicked queen summoned her huntsman.

"Take Snow White to the deepest part of the forest and kill her," she ordered.

The huntsman was a kind man. He didn't want to harm Snow White, so he took her into the forest and left her there.

It was getting dark and Snow White felt very frightened. She looked around for a way out and saw a path running through the trees. It led to a little house.

Snow White tapped on the door. It swung open, so she stepped inside. In the middle of the room was a little table set with seven little plates, seven little knives and forks and seven little cups. Around the table were seven little chairs.

Snow White called out, but there was no one home.

Tired and hungry, Snow White ate some food from one of the plates
and drank from one of the cups, then she went upstairs and lay down.
She was fast asleep when the owners of the house came home. They
were seven little dwarves who had been working all day in the hills.

"Someone has been in our house," they said and all began talking
at once. Their voices woke Snow White. She sat up in bed and rubbed
her eyes.

When the dwarves heard Snow White's story they felt sorry for her.
"You can stay here as long as you like," they told her.

Snow White loved living with the dwarves. They took good care of her and in return she cleaned the house and cooked their meals.

"You will be safe here, but never let anyone into the house while we are away," they told her.

Back in the palace, the wicked queen thought that Snow White was dead. She asked the mirror if she was now the most beautiful in the land.

The mirror answered. "Oh, queen, your beauty is so rare. Yet, Snow White living in the woods is a thousand times more fair!"

This made the queen angrier than ever.

"I will get rid of Snow White myself," she vowed.

The queen put on a bonnet and a white apron and filled a basket with the shiniest, rosiest apples she could find. Then she went to the house in the forest and knocked on the door.

"Buy my lovely apples," she said to Snow White.

Snow White forgot what the dwarves had told her.

"I would love to buy an apple,' she said.

The evil queen picked out the reddest, juiciest apple.

"Taste it, my dear," she said, smiling wickedly, for the apple was poisoned. Snow White took a bite of the apple and she fell to the ground.

"That is the end of you," cackled the queen and she left.

When the dwarves came home and saw Snow White lying so still they began to cry. They thought she was dead.

"It must be the work of the wicked queen," they sobbed.

The dwarves dressed Snow White in her prettiest dress, put flowers in her hair and laid her in a glass case.

"Now everyone can admire her beauty," they said.

The dwarves took it in turns to watch over Snow White. Later that day, a handsome prince rode past. When he saw Snow White he immediately fell in love with her.

"I have never seen anyone more beautiful," he said. "Allow me to gaze on her beauty."

The dwarves lifted the glass case and the prince held Snow White in his arms and kissed her gently on the lips. As if by magic, Snow White opened her eyes.

"Where am I?" she asked.

The prince took her hand in his.

"You are safe with me," he told her.

At the palace, the queen couldn't wait to ask her magic mirror, "Mirror, mirror, on the wall, who is the fairest of them all?"

The mirror answered, "Oh, queen, your beauty is so rare, but Snow White is the one that is more fair."

The queen's face darkened with anger and in a terrible rage, she picked up the magic mirror and threw it across the room. It hit the wall and smashed into a thousand jagged pieces.

Then the wicked, jealous queen stormed out of the palace forever.

The prince asked Snow White to marry him. He took her back
to his palace. The seven dwarves were overjoyed that their friend had
found happiness.

"You must come and live at the palace, too," Snow White told them.
"You will never have to work again."

Snow White and her handsome prince made a lovely couple and the
seven dwarves were their guests of honour at their wonderful wedding.
No one saw or heard of the jealous queen again and Snow White and
the prince lived happily ever after.

The Frog Prince

Once upon a time, there was a beautiful, but spoilt princess. Her father, the king, bought her anything she wanted. The princess had a wardrobe full of beautiful dresses and a bedroom full of expensive toys. Her favourite was a shiny golden ball and every day, she played with it in the palace gardens.

One day, the princess dropped the golden ball into the royal pond. "I want my golden ball back!" she cried as she stomped her feet.

"I'll fetch your ball, Princess," said a small voice. It belonged to a little, green frog who was sitting on a lilypad.

"I'll fetch your ball if you'll let me eat from your plate, drink from your cup, sleep in your bed and give me a kiss," said the frog.

The spoilt princess didn't think it mattered if she made a promise and didn't keep it.

"I promise I'll eat with you, let you sleep in my bed and I'll give you a kiss," she said. "Just get my ball!"

The frog dived into the royal pond. Moments later, he reappeared with the golden ball in his mouth. The princess took the ball and ran off without even saying thank you.

The next day, the princess and her father sat down to a huge banquet. There was every kind of food imaginable – piles of pies, mountains of sweets treats and hundreds of delicious cakes.

As the princess was about to tuck into her second cupcake, there was a faint knocking on the door of the banquet hall.

It was the little, green frog.

"You promised I could eat from your plate, princess," he croaked.

"Ugh!" said the princess. "I don't want to eat with you. You're a slimy, warty frog!"

The king looked sternly at his daughter.

"That frog helped you when you were in need," he said. "If you make a promise, you should keep it."

The frog hopped up onto the table and ate from the princess's special gold plate. He gobbled all the ice cream and took the last ham sandwich.

When the king threw raisins in the air, the frog caught them in mid-air with his long, sticky tongue. The king roared with laughter, but the princess didn't find it funny at all.

At the end of the meal, the frog gave a big burp. He hopped over to the princess and croaked, "Now you must take me up to your room, so we can have a sleepover."

"Ugh, Daddy, do I have to?" the princess asked the king.

"You gave your word," replied the king. "Princesses do not break their promises."

So, the princess picked up the cold and slippery frog and took him to her bedroom in the highest tower. She put the frog down in the corner of the room, but he leapt on to one of her nice clean royal pillows. He stretched out, yawned, and fell asleep.

The princess climbed into the big golden bed beside the frog and tried to sleep. Just as she was nodding off, the frog began to snore. It was a big, croaky, rattling kind of snore. The princess clamped a pillow around her head, but she couldn't block out the horrible sound!

All night, the princess lay awake, unable to sleep. When morning came, she felt so tired. She could hardly keep her eyes open, but the frog had slept for hours and was wide awake!

"It is time I left," said the frog and the princess felt very glad. "But first, you must fulfil the last part of your promise," croaked the frog. "You must give me a kiss."

So, she pursed her lips, leaned over and gave the frog a big kiss.

As the princess kissed the frog, he suddenly began to glow. The princess stepped back and watched as the frog shimmered, glimmered and slowly began to change.

Suddenly, there was a shower of bright stars and in the frog's place stood a handsome young man.

"I am a prince who was enchanted by an evil witch," he said. "I was doomed to stay a frog until I found a princess who would kiss me. You have freed me from the spell!"

The princess thought the prince was very handsome.

"I've learnt my lesson and will never need anything to make me happy, other than you," she said.

The prince and princess kissed and decided to spend the rest of their lives together.

Tom Thumb

Once, there lived a man and a woman who longed for a child. Every day, they would listen to the little children who ran around outside their garden.

"I wish we had children to fill our lives with fun," said the woman. "Just one child would be enough to make me happy. Even a really small one, no bigger than my thumb."

A few months later, her strange wish came true. She had a baby boy who was perfect in every way, but was as tiny as a mouse.

The man and his wife gave the boy as much food as they could afford. Yet, no matter how much he ate, he grew no bigger than his mother's thumb. So, the man and the wife called their son Tom Thumb.

Although he was small, Tom was clever and he loved to help his parents around the house. He could squeeze into small spaces and sweep out the dust or sew up the holes in their clothes with tiny stitches.

Each day, Tom helped in the garden. He pulled up weeds and planted seeds, but when it was time to go to the forest to cut wood, Tom's father told him to stay behind.

"I don't want to stay behind," thought Tom. When his father wasn't looking, Tom crept into his father's pocket to hide. As soon as they got into the woods, Tom gave his father a fright by shouting up to him.

"Hello Dad, I'm here in your pocket."

Tom's father was cross, but he didn't stay angry for long. He fished Tom out of his pocket and sat him on a twig while he chopped wood.

As they laughed and chatted together, two strangers came walking through the woods. Hearing the talking, they wandered into the clearing and saw Tom talking to his father.

"We could make a fortune if we put that tiny boy in a show," whispered one of the men.

"People would come from all over the world to see him," agreed his friend. The strangers offered Tom's father a bag of gold in exchange for Tom.

"My son is more precious than all the gold in the world," said Tom's father proudly. Tom climbed on to his father's shoulder and whispered in his ear.

"You are very poor, Father. Take the gold and let me go. I'll be back before bedtime."

After much persuasion, Tom's father agreed and one of the strangers gave him a bulging bag of gold coins..

The man sat Tom Thumb on the brim of his hat so he could see the countryside as they travelled. They walked for several miles before they stopped to rest.

"Please put me down so I can take a nap," said Tom. "All this travelling has made me tired."

Placing Tom on a large leaf, the man and his friend lay back in the warm grass and were soon snoring loudly. Tom jumped up and ran away. When he heard the men searching for him, he hid down a rabbit hole.

As it got dark the two men gave up and went away. Tom had escaped but he was far from home.

Tom walked and walked but his steps were so tiny that he didn't get very far. Exhausted, he settled down in an empty snail shell to sleep. Just as he was dozing off, he heard loud voices. Two thieves were arguing about the best way to break into a house.

"Pick the lock and creep in quietly," suggested one thief.

"No," said the other, "let's smash a window, grab what we can and run."

"I can help," shouted Tom as loudly as he could. One of the thieves picked up the shell and they stared in amazement at the tiny boy.

The thieves took Tom to the house and watched him squeezed through a small gap under the door. "Climb up to the window and undo the lock," they whispered.

Instead, Tom started banging pots and pans and shouting as loudly as he could. "Sssh!" said the thieves. "Be quiet or we'll get caught."

"You mustn't rob this house!" cried Tom, banging the pans even louder.

There was the sound of footsteps upstairs and a light turned on.

"Who's there!" shouted an angry voice. The thieves were so frightened they ran away into the woods.

The man who owned the house was surprised to find a tiny boy sitting in his kitchen. Tom Thumb introduced himself and explained that he had scared the thieves off.

The man was so grateful that he offered Tom a reward, but all Tom wanted was to go home. The man was happy to help and they set off at once on his horse and cart.

When they reached a little cottage near the woods, Tom called out. "I'm home!"

Tom's parents cried with joy and Tom hugged them tight and promised never to leave home again.

Hansel and Gretel

Long ago, by a dark wood, lived a poor woodcutter who had two children called Hansel and Gretel. Even though they were poor, the children were happy. Every day they played in the woods and fed their bird friends in the forest.

One day, the woodcutter said, "I am bringing a stepmother home to live with us. I want you to love her as much as you love me."

Hansel and Gretel hugged him.

"We will try, Father," they said.

However, the stepmother was mean and cruel. She wanted the woodcutter to get rid of Hansel and Gretel, so she could have him all to herself.

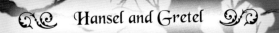

"We are so very poor and there isn't enough food to go round," she said to him one day. "The next time you go into the woods, you must take Hansel and Gretel and leave them there."

"What will become of them?" asked the woodcutter sadly.

"Don't worry," replied the sly stepmother. "They're old enough to look after themselves. They'll be just fine."

Hansel overheard his stepmother and decided to make a plan.
He filled his pockets with crusts of bread and when they went into the
woods, he dropped a trail of breadcrumbs on the ground.

When their father had finished cutting wood, he turned to his
Hansel and Gretel.

"Wait here," he said sadly. "I will be back shortly."

Then he kissed them and left.

Hansel and Gretel waited and waited, but their father didn't
come back.

"Don't worry," said Hansel, "I've left a trail of breadcrumbs that will lead us home."

When Hansel looked, the breadcrumbs had vanished.

"The birds must have eaten it," he said and Gretel began to cry.

Then, Hansel noticed a little house behind the trees. Its roof was made of gingerbread and its walls were made of cake. The window frames were striped sugar candy and the door was made of chocolate.

The children were very hungry, so they broke off some of the cake from the walls.

"Mmm. It's delicious," they said.

Suddenly, the door swung open and a sweet, old lady appeared.

"Come in, children," said the old lady. Hansel and Gretel stepped inside, but the door slammed behind them. "You are my prisoners now," said the woman, who was really a witch.

The witch cackled as she locked Hansel in a large cage and made Gretel do all the housework. She fed the children lots of sweets. At first they tasted nice, but soon Hansel and Gretel got tired of eating so much sugary food.

"Why does she keep feeding us?" asked Gretel.

That night Gretel overheard the witch talking in her sleep.

"I will have plump children for my supper soon," she mumbled.

Gretel told Hansel what the witch had said. So, when she came to test how plump Hansel's finger was, he held out a bony twig. The witch had bad eyesight so she didn't notice.

"I won't eat you today," she said.

Soon, however, the witch grew tired of waiting.

"Maybe I'll have both of you for supper tomorrow," she hissed. "Light the fire under the oven, Gretel, I want it to be good and hot for tomorrow," she said and went to bed.

"We must do something," whispered Hansel to Gretel.

The next day, the fire blazed under the oven.

"I want you to check if it's big enough to fit both of you," said the witch, opening the oven door.

"How do I do that?" asked Gretel.

"Get inside, of course," said the sly witch.

Gretel looked at the oven. "Will you show me how?" she asked.

The witch couldn't resist showing off. She hitched up her skirts and climbed in. Quick as a flash, Gretel slammed the door.

"Let me out," screamed the witch, but Gretel ignored her. She rushed across the kitchen and freed Hansel.

They ran outside and their little bird friends flew down from the
trees. They led the children along the winding forest paths, back home
to the woodcutter's cottage.

When their father saw them he was overjoyed, "I realised that your
stepmother was wicked and I sent her away," he said.

Hansel and Gretel hugged their father. They went back to their
happy, simple life and were never troubled by the wicked witch again.

Four Skilled Brothers

Long ago, four brothers set off to seek their fortunes along four different roads. On the first road, the eldest brother met a hunter.

"I will teach you how to be quick and cunning, so you can sneak around quietly without being caught," said the hunter. So, the eldest brother went with the hunter and learned how to be quick and cunning.

The second brother met an astronomer.

"I will show you the secrets of the stars and you shall have this fine magic telescope," said the astronomer. So, the second brother went with the astronomer and learned how to use the telescope.

The third brother met a magician. He promised that he would show him how to make a person vanish into thin air. So, the third brother agreed to go with the magician and learn all about magic.

The youngest brother met a tailor who was looking for an apprentice. He promised to teach the brother everything he knew. So, the youngest brother went with the tailor. He taught him how to make fine clothes and gave him a magic needle that could sew any two things together.

When the four brothers had learned their skills, they returned home. Each one wondered how he might put his skills to good use.

One morning, a messenger arrived. The king's daughter had been snatched by a fierce dragon.

"The king is offering a large reward to whoever can free the princess," said the messenger. The four brothers agreed at once that they must rescue the king's daughter.

The brother who had become an astronomer looked through his magic telescope. He searched all over the world. Finally he spotted the princess and the dragon on a rocky island far out at sea.

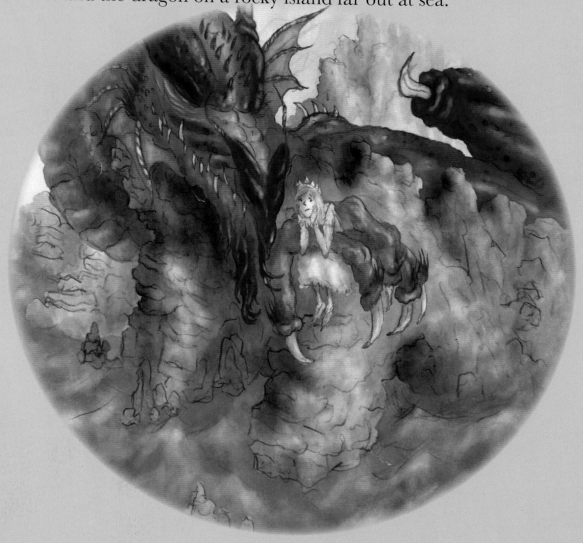

The four brothers took a ship and set sail for the island. When they drew near, the astronomer looked through his telescope again.

"The dragon is asleep with his head on the princess's lap," he said.

"Don't worry," said the brother who had learned to be quick and cunning. "I know what to do."

He climbed out of the ship and crept close to the sleeping dragon. He lifted its scaly head and silently picked up the princess. He took her back to the ship, but just as it was setting off, the dragon awoke.

Roaring with anger, the dragon stretched out its powerful wings and flew after them. No matter how fast they sailed, the dragon flew faster, breathing fire and smoke.

The brother who'd learned to be a magician waved his wand and made the dragon disappear.

Just then, there was a huge crash as the ship hit some rocks. The magic wand fell into the sea and the ship began to sink below the waves. The four brothers and the princess grabbed the splintered planks to keep afloat in the rough waves.

"We're going to drown!" cried the frightened princess.

At last, the sea became calmer.

"Who will save us?" asked the princess.

"I haven't used my skills yet," said the youngest brother, who had trained to be a tailor.

He gathered all the bits of ragged sail and began to sew them with his magic needle. Before long, there was enough to cover all the floating planks and make a little boat. Everyone began to paddle and soon, they reached land.

News spread quickly that the four brothers had rescued the princess. A golden royal carriage came to pick them up and they rode through the streets to shouts and cheers.

The king was so delighted to have his daughter safely home, he commanded that there would be a special celebration throughout the kingdom. For the first time in ages the palace was filled with laughter. Everyone danced and feasted.

The king was so impressed by the skills that the brothers had used to save his daughter, he gave each of them a place in the royal household. The first brother became the royal hunter, the second became the royal astronomer, the brother who had become a magician entertained everyone at royal parties. As for the fourth brother, he made a beautiful wedding dress for the princess and they were married soon after.

The brothers had used their skills for good and they all lived long and happy lives.

Little Red Riding Hood

Once there was a little girl who lived on the edge of a deep, dark wood. Her grandmother had given her a long, red cloak with a hood. She liked the cloak so much and wore it so often that everyone called her Little Red Riding Hood.

One day, Little Red Riding Hood's mother was baking some cupcakes in the kitchen.

"Can you take a basket of these cakes to Grandma's house?" she said. "Grandma is poorly and I'm sure they will cheer her up. It's a long way, so make sure you stay on the path and don't talk to strangers."

Little Red Riding Hood put on her red cloak and her mother filled the basket with the freshly baked cakes. She kissed her mother goodbye and set off, but before she reached the forest path, her mother called out.

"Remember what I said, always stay on the path and never talk to strangers." Then she waved and went back inside.

Little Red Riding Hood nodded and waved back as she set off into the deep, dark wood.

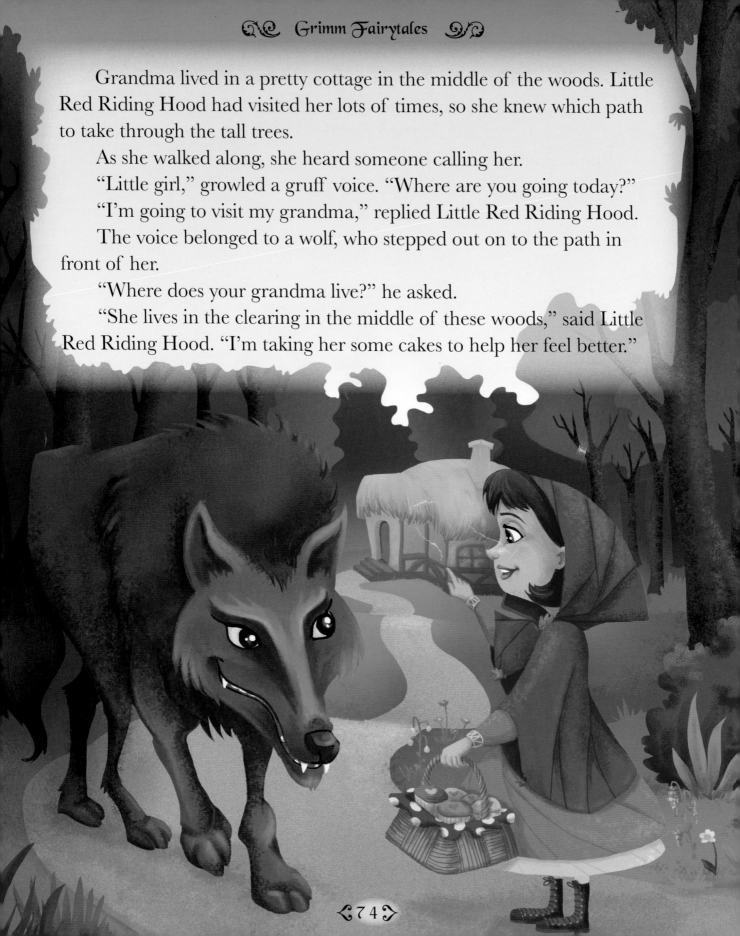

Grandma lived in a pretty cottage in the middle of the woods. Little Red Riding Hood had visited her lots of times, so she knew which path to take through the tall trees.

As she walked along, she heard someone calling her.

"Little girl," growled a gruff voice. "Where are you going today?"

"I'm going to visit my grandma," replied Little Red Riding Hood.

The voice belonged to a wolf, who stepped out on to the path in front of her.

"Where does your grandma live?" he asked.

"She lives in the clearing in the middle of these woods," said Little Red Riding Hood. "I'm taking her some cakes to help her feel better."

The wolf licked his lips. He'd much rather eat a little girl than a cake. So, he thought carefully and came up with a cunning plan.

"If your grandma is ill you should take her some flowers," he suggested. "There are lots of pretty ones growing here that are sure to make her smile."

Little Red Riding Hood thought this was a great idea and immediately started picking a bunch of the most beautiful blooms. While she was busy, the wolf ran all the way to Grandma's house.

When he got there, he locked poor Grandma in a cupboard. Grabbing one of her nightdresses and a nightcap, he quickly closed the curtains and jumped into bed.

Just than, Little Red Riding Hood knocked on the door.

"Come in, dear," said the wolf, trying to sound like Grandma.

"You must have a very sore throat," said Little Red Riding Hood, kindly. She put down the basket of cakes and walked towards the bed to give her grandma a kiss. As she got closer, she noticed something strange.

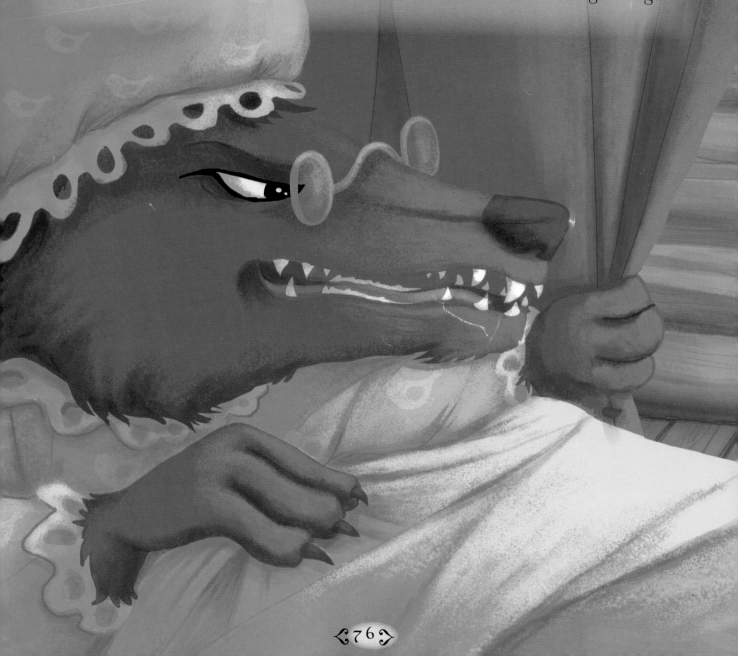

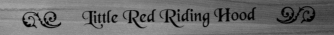

"Grandma, what big ears you have," said Little Red Riding Hood.
"All the better to hear you with," replied the wolf in a squeaky voice.
Little Red Riding Hood took a step closer.
"Grandma, what big eyes you have," she said.
"All the better to see you with," said the wolf.
She moved closer still and peered into her grandma's face.
"Grandma, what big , sharp teeth you have!"

"All the better to EAT you with," said the wolf, leaping out of bed. There was a terrible commotion as he chased poor Little Red Riding Hood all over Grandma's cottage.

Luckily, a kind woodcutter was passing by. He heard the terrible banging and crashing.

"I bet that wolf is up to no good again," he said. He raised his sharp axe and burst in. "I fancy a nice bit of wolf for my supper!" he cried.

When the wolf heard this, he ran off yelping into the forest, never to be seen again.

Just then, Little Red Riding Hood heard a knocking sound coming from the cupboard. She opened the door and found Grandma inside.

"I'm glad that nasty wolf is gone," she said. "He was very rude."

Grandma hugged Little Red Riding Hood and thanked the brave woodcutter. They all sat down and had hot drinks and some of the delicious cakes that Little Red Riding Hood had brought.

After that, Little Red Riding Hood never wandered off the forest path and she never talked to strangers ever again.

Rapunzel

Once upon a time, there was a wicked witch who had a beautiful garden full of fruit trees. Next door lived a man whose wife longed to taste the fruit from the witch's garden.

"Please get one for me," she begged. "If I don't eat that fruit I will waste away."

Her husband knew that the garden belonged to a witch, but his wife asked him so many times that at last he gave in.

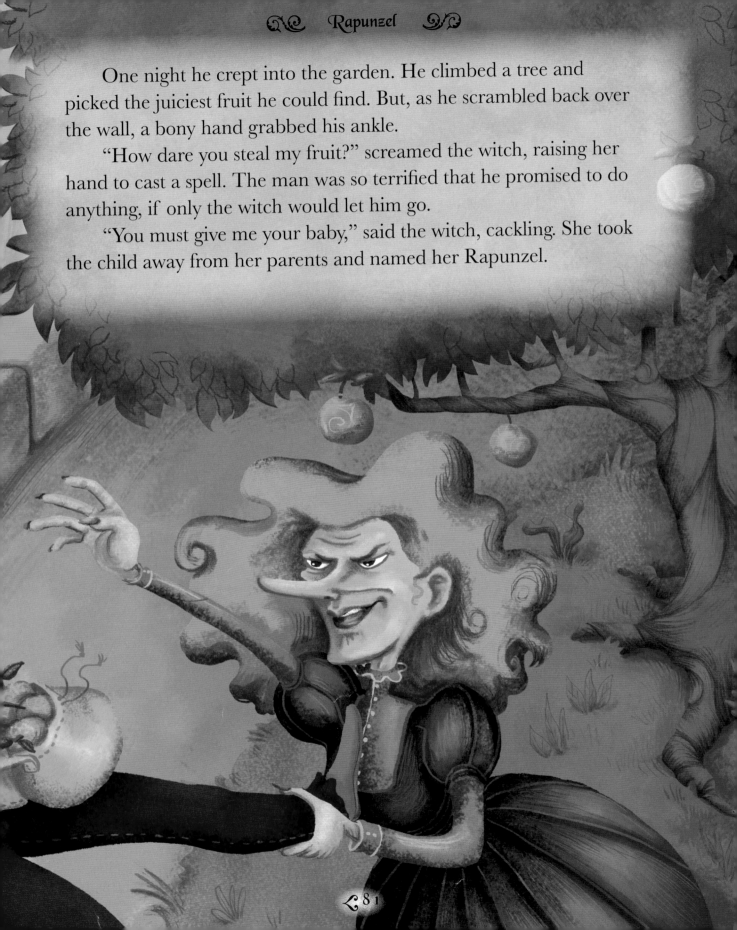

One night he crept into the garden. He climbed a tree and picked the juiciest fruit he could find. But, as he scrambled back over the wall, a bony hand grabbed his ankle.

"How dare you steal my fruit?" screamed the witch, raising her hand to cast a spell. The man was so terrified that he promised to do anything, if only the witch would let him go.

"You must give me your baby," said the witch, cackling. She took the child away from her parents and named her Rapunzel.

The witch locked Rapunzel in a tall tower with no doors and only one window. Over time, she grew into a beautiful young woman with long, golden hair.

When the witch wanted to visit Rapunzel, she stood at the bottom of the tower and called out, "Rapunzel, Rapunzel, let down your hair."

Then the young woman would hang her hair out of the window for the witch to climb up.

One day, when Rapunzel was all alone, a prince rode by on his horse. He heard her singing and was so enchanted that he stayed to listen. When the witch came to visit, the prince hid behind a bush.

The prince watched in wonder as the witch called out, "Rapunzel, Rapunzel, let down your hair."

He saw Rapunzel drop her hair out of the window and instantly fell in love. The prince waited until the witch had gone and then stood at the bottom of the tower.

"Rapunzel, Rapunzel, let down your hair," he shouted, trying to make his voice sound like the witch's.

Rapunzel hung her hair out of the window. She was shocked when a handsome prince climbed up instead of the witch, but he was so charming and kind that she soon fell in love with him.

The prince visited every day. Each time he brought a ball of silk thread with him and Rapunzel set to work weaving it into a ladder. When it was almost long enough for her to escape she heard the witch approaching and quickly hid it away.

As the witch climbed up her hair, Rapunzel couldn't help complaining that she was much heavier than the handsome prince.

The witch flew into a rage. She grabbed a pair of scissors and chopped off Rapunzel's long hair. Then, she took her out into the wilderness and left her there all alone.

The witch returned to the tower and waited for the prince. It wasn't long before he arrived and called out to his true love, "Rapunzel, Rapunzel, let down your hair."

The witch threw down the hair she had cut from Rapunzel and the prince climbed up. When he saw the witch at the window he yelled out in fright.

"She's gone," the witch screamed, "and you will never find her."

Horrified, the prince let go of the hair and fell into a tangle of bushes. The sharp thorns tore at his clothes and scratched him. He staggered away, broken hearted.

For days the prince searched for his lost love. He called her name but all he heard was the wind in the trees and the birds singing. Their sweet voices reminded him of Rapunzel and he felt sad and alone.

At last, he stumbled into a wild place where no trees grew and no birds sang. He sank to the ground to rest but a beautiful sound made him jump to his feet.

A bright clear voice was singing the saddest song he had ever heard. It was Rapunzel. When she saw her prince she cried with joy.

The prince took Rapunzel home to his palace and they were married the following day. Everyone in the kingdom celebrated the royal wedding. The streets were decorated with flags and streamers and everyone danced, sang and had fabulous feasts. No one was as joyful as the prince and his new bride, Rapunzel. They lived happily ever after.

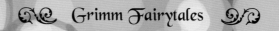

The Brave Little Tailor

There once was a tailor who worked hard to make fine clothes. He was very small, so everyone thought he must be timid and weak. "He couldn't harm a fly," they said, laughing. The little tailor didn't think it was fair that the villagers called him timid.

One sunny day the little tailor opened his window while he ate lunch. A cloud of flies buzzed into the room. They swarmed around his plate and crawled all over the bread and jam. The tailor swatted them away and knocked seven of the flies to the floor. The others flew off in fright.

Impressed by what he had done, the tailor set to work making himself a belt with the words, "Seven in one blow," sewn on to it. He wore it as he walked around the village and rumors of his bravery soon began to spread.

"I heard he trapped seven rats," said one of his neighbors.

"No it was wild boars," replied another.

Within a week word had got around that the little tailor had beaten seven dragons with one hand. When the local giant heard this tale he was very angry.

"I am the most powerful in the land," he roared. "We'll soon find out if this tailor is as strong as me."

One day, the giant strode through the village to the tailor's house and challenged him to a contest. The giant picked up a boulder that was lying nearby and squeezed it between his huge fingers. The tailor watched in dismay as water ran out of the boulder.

"Your turn," bellowed the giant. "If you're so strong, let's see you squeeze water from a rock."

"The rocks out here aren't hard enough," said the tailor. "I have the perfect one inside."

He dashed into his house, grabbed an old sponge and held it under the tap. He carried the sodden sponge outside and squeezed it hard.

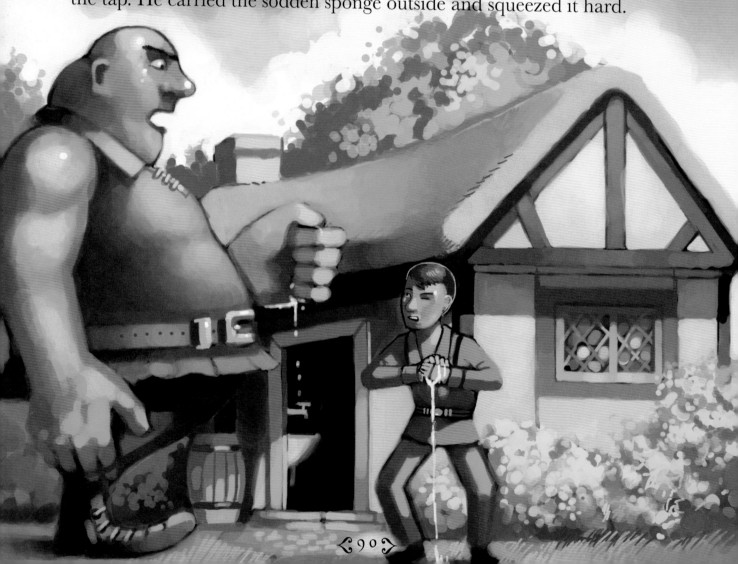

The giant gasped as water ran out of the tailor's tiny hand.

"Well, you won't be able to beat me in a throwing competition!" the giant boomed.

He picked up a stone and tossed it into the air with the swing of his massive arm. It soared through the clouds and out of sight. Eventually they heard the stone land with a thud.

When the tailor went to pick it up he spotted a grey bird sitting on the ground.

Without the giant seeing, he gently picked up the bird instead. "My rock will go so far that it will never come down," he boasted. He lifted his arm and let the bird go. It flew off into the sky and disappeared.

"I'm impressed, but not impressed enough to believe that you can beat me," said the giant. "Let's see who can push this cart the farthest."

"I'll go first," said the tailor. Then, leaning down to take off the brake, he placed his shoulder against the cart and pushed with all his might. The road from the tailor's house was on a slight slope, so the cart rolled easily downhill.

When he got to the bottom the tailor secretly put the brake back on. The giant leaned his enormous shoulder against the cart and gave it a shove. It didn't budge. He pushed with all his strength but could not make the cart move.

"Now it's my turn to come up with a challenge," said the tailor. "Can you jump over this tree?"

The giant bent his big knees and tried to spring up in the air, but he was so heavy his feet barely lifted off the ground.

When it was the tailor's turn he asked the giant to reach up and bend one of the branches down for him. The giant was keen to see the tiny tailor leap over the tree, so he did as he was asked. The tailor held on tight to the end of the branch. When the giant let go, it sprang back up flinging him over the top of the tree to land on the other side.

Roaring with frustration, the giant pulled the tree out of the ground.

"I may not be able to jump over a tree, but I can carry one," he said growling.

"So can I," said the tailor. "You hold the trunk and I'll lift the branches up."

The giant tucked the tree's trunk under one immense arm while the tailor skipped round behind him and climbed up into the branches.

"This is easy," he called out.

"It's heavier than I thought," said the giant, grunting. He tried to glance behind but he couldn't see anything through the leafy branches.

Soon, the giant was too tired to hold the tree up any longer and he dropped it on the ground. By the time he had turned around, the tailor had jumped down from the branches and was lifting up a twig with one hand.

"What shall we do next?" the tailor asked with a smile.

The weary giant shook his huge head.

"I give up, you are the strongest in the land," he admitted. "I'm going for a lie down."

The ground shook as the giant plodded off, yawning and grumbling to himself.

The tailor went back home, whistling happily. After that, the villagers never made fun of him again.

Rumpelstiltskin

Long ago, there was a poor man who visited a wicked king. The man was so nervous and wanted to impress the king so much he told him that his daughter could spin straw into golden thread. The king was very greedy. He made the man bring his daughter to the palace. Then the king took her to a room full of straw.

"You must spin this straw into gold by morning, or you will die," he said.

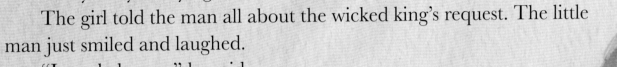

The poor girl was very frightened. She didn't know how to spin straw into gold and she began to cry.

Suddenly, a strange little man appeared. He was dressed in green from top to toe and had a long red beard.

"Why are you crying?" he asked.

The girl told the man all about the wicked king's request. The little man just smiled and laughed.

"I can help you," he said.

The little man jumped up and down with excitement.

"What will you give me if I do it for you?" he asked.

The girl offered him her necklace and he skipped over to the spinning wheel. Overnight, he spun every stalk of straw into long golden thread. When he had finished, he snatched the necklace and disappeared.

The girl was still staring in amazement at the mounds of gold when the king arrived. That night, the delighted king wanted the girl to spin even more straw.

"You know what will happen if you don't," he said.

Once again, the girl was left alone.

"I cannot spin straw into gold," she said and she began to cry. Just as the tears began to trickle down her face, the little man appeared.

"What will you give me if I spin this straw into gold?" he asked.

The girl took a ring off her finger and held it out to him. Grabbing it quickly, the man hopped over to the spinning wheel. He spun all night and transformed the yellow straw into shining gold.

At daybreak he vanished, just as he had done the morning before.

The king was amazed when he saw the heaps of glistening gold thread. He took the girl into a room filled with even more straw.

"Turn all of this into gold and I will make you my wife," he said.

For a third time the strange little man appeared in the room. This time, when he asked the girl what she would give him for turning the straw into gold, she had nothing left to offer him.

"Then you must promise to give me your first child," he said and swiftly started spinning. Before daybreak, all the straw had been spun into gold.

The king kept his promise. He married the girl and made her his queen.

The following year a beautiful baby was born. The queen could not have been happier. Then, one evening as she laid the baby in its cot the little man appeared.

"Give me what you promised," he demanded.

The queen cried and begged him not to take her child. She offered him all the treasure in the kingdom, but the little man did not want gold.

"If you can guess my name you can keep your baby," he laughed. "You have three days to try."

On the first day, the queen wrote a list of every name she knew. The little man laughed as she read each one out.

"You'll never guess my name!" he cried as he disappeared in a puff of smoke.

The next day, the queen sent a messenger to gather every name in the kingdom. Once again, she read the list to the strange little man.

"Is it Birdbrain, Beetlebug or Crumchucker?" she asked.

The little man howled with laughter and jumped up and down.

"No, no, NO!" he replied.

Then, on the third and final day, a messenger returned with a strange story to tell.

"High up in the hills, I saw a funny little man dancing round a fire and singing a strange song."

"Tonight I dance and magic I make. Tomorrow the boy child will I take. No knows my clever game, that Rumpelstiltskin is my name!"

The queen waited for the little man to appear. As before, she read out all sorts of names. The man laughed at each one until the queen read out the last name on her list.

"Then your name must be RUMPELSTILTSKIN!"

The little man was furious. He stamped his foot and screamed. Suddenly, he disappeared in a puff of smoke.

After that, Rumpelstiltskin was never seen again and everyone lived happily ever after.

The Golden Goose

O nce upon a time there was a woodcutter who had three sons. The two older sons were very clever and proud. They thought their younger brother, Hans, wasn't nearly as clever as they were.

One day the eldest brother went into the forest to chop wood, with some bread and ham from his mother. A little old man saw him and asked if he could spare something to eat.

"Go away," said the eldest brother. "If I give you my food, I won't have any for myself."

The eldest brother went to chop down a tree, but a branch fell on his arm and he had to return home.

The next day, the middle brother went out to chop wood, with some bread and cheese that his mother had given him. He too met the little old man.

"Can you spare some food?" the man asked.

"Leave me alone," said the middle brother. "Why should I give you any food?"

When the middle brother tried to cut down a tree, a branch fell on his foot and he had to return home with no wood.

On the third day, Hans travelled far into the forest to chop wood. He also met the little old man who asked him for a bite to eat.

"You are welcome to share all that I have," said Hans.

The old man ate the food and thanked Hans.

"For your reward, chop down that big oak tree over there," he said.

Hans chopped down the tree and to is amazement, inside was a goose with golden feathers.

"Carry the goose and journey through the forest," said the old man, before he suddenly disappeared.

Hans carried the goose through the forest. Before long, he came to an inn. It was nearly dark so Hans decided to stay for the night.

That night, the innkeeper's eldest daughter saw the golden goose.

"Nobody will notice if I take just one of its golden feathers," she thought. When the girl tried to pluck a golden feather, she found she couldn't let go of the goose.

The goose was magic, and her hand was stuck for good!

She called for her sister.

"Grab me and pull me off this goose," she said, "and we will have a golden feather!" But when her sister grabbed her, she found she was stuck too.

The innkeeper's third daughter came down to see what all the fuss was about. Before she knew it, she was stuck to the second sister.

The next morning, Hans came down to find the three sisters stuck together. He pretended not to notice them, picked up the goose and left the inn. The sisters had no choice but to follow him. As Hans walked away, the innkeeper saw him.

"Hey!" he cried "Where are you all going!"

He grabbed the youngest sister, and found that he too was stuck fast.

Hans thought it was very funny. He walked all day, with the innkeeper and his daughters stuck behind him, puffing and panting.

Along the way, they met a rich merchant.

"If you sell me that goose," the merchant said, "I will give you fifty pieces of gold."

As soon as the merchant touched the innkeeper, he too was stuck fast to the line!

Hans walked happily along with the goose, not caring at all about the people that were following him. As they reached a field, the merchant called to two farm workers.

"Come save me from this magic goose!"

The two ploughmen rushed up to help the merchant. As soon as they touched him, they joined the chain.

Hans didn't care. He just strolled on, whistling happily, until he reached a great city.

In this city there was an enormous grey castle, where a king lived with his only daughter. The king's daughter was the saddest person alive.

The king had tried everything to make her happy.

"I will give half my kingdom to anyone who can make my daughter laugh," he said. Many clowns and jesters performed in front of the princess, but she never laughed at any of them.

That day, ouside the palace, the princess saw Hans marching past, happily along carrying the golden goose. Behind him were the three sisters, an innkeeper, a merchant and two ploughmen puffing and panting behind him!

The princess couldn't believe her eyes.

"That's the silliest thing I've ever seen!" she said. Her smile turned into a snort, then a giggle, and finally she laughed!

When the princess and Hans met, they fell in love. The goose was so happy that she fluttered her feathers and the seven people were released. They fell over in a big heap, and everyone laughed even more.

Hans and the princess were soon married and lived together, happily ever after.

Cinderella

There was once a girl called Cinderella who lived with her cruel stepmother and two nasty stepsisters. Poor Cinderella was treated like a servant. She did all the washing, cooking and cleaning while her stepsisters lazed around or went out to shop for the latest fashions.

Cinderella wore a ragged old dress and her stepsisters loved making fun of how tattered and shabby she looked. Even with the finest clothes and hours spent combing and curling their hair, the stepsisters could never look as beautiful as Cinderella.

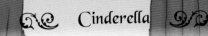

One day an invitation arrived from the palace. The prince was throwing a grand ball and he had invited Cinderella and her stepsisters.

"Of course you won't be able to go, Cinderella," her stepmother told her nastily. "You'll be much too busy helping your sisters get ready."

"The prince wouldn't want someone as scruffy as you at his royal party," sneered one of the stepsisters.

"Now polish my purple shoes and make sure my jewelry is super sparkly," ordered the other stepsister, stuffing a chocolate in her mouth.

Cinderella was heartbroken. On the day of the ball she spent hours helping her stepsisters get ready and when they had left, she sat down and cried.

With a fizzle and a flash a kindly old woman appeared in front of her.

"I am your fairy godmother," she said. "Why are you crying?"

"I wish I could go to the ball," said Cinderella, sobbing.

The fairy godmother asked her to fetch a pumpkin. Cinderella was puzzled but she did as she was told and returned with the biggest pumpkin she could find. With a wave of her wand the fairy godmother turned the pumpkin into a golden carriage.

Cinderella watched in amazement as her fairy godmother changed six little mice into horses to pull the golden carriage. Then she turned a rat into a coachman and two lizards into smartly dressed footmen.

"You shall go to the ball," she cried.

Cinderella looked down at her ragged dress and sighed.

"Thank you, but I can't go looking like this."

"Of course not," agreed her fairy godmother and she waved her wand again. Cinderella gasped as her dress became a splendid ball gown made from pink silk and covered in jewels. Magical, dainty glass slippers appeared on her feet.

"Have a wonderful time," her godmother said. "But you must be home by midnight, that's when the spell wears off."

When Cinderella arrived at the ball, all the guests turned to stare. She looked so beautiful no one recognized her, not even her own stepsisters.

"She must be a princess," they whispered. "Look at her dazzling dress and stylish shoes."

The prince was enchanted by Cinderella's beauty and asked her to dance. They whirled round the room and danced all night.

The evening flew by and Cinderella was so happy dancing and laughing with the prince that she forgot to keep an eye on the time.

When the palace clock began to strike midnight, she gasped in horror. The prince must not see her beautiful ball gown turn back into the ragged old dress.

Cinderella said goodbye and dashed down the palace steps towards her golden carriage. She was in such a hurry that one of her glass slippers fell off and was left behind.

The next day the prince declared that he was in love with the mystery guest and wished to marry her. He had found Cinderella's glass slipper and planned to try it on every lady in the land until he found her.

The prince rode from house to house searching for his true love, but when he arrived at the stepmother's door she quickly shoved Cinderella into the garden.

The stepsisters took turns trying to squeeze a foot into the tiny glass slipper, but their toes were too big and would not fit inside.

The prince was about to give up and move on to the next house when he spotted Cinderella in the garden.

"Who is that?" he asked at once.

"Oh, she's just a serving girl," lied the stepmother.

But the prince demanded that Cinderella be brought inside to try on the slipper. She smiled at him shyly and slid her foot perfectly into the slipper.

Laughing with joy, the prince swept Cinderella into his arms. She gladly agreed to marry him and they lived happily ever after.

Snow White and Rose Red

Once upon a time there were two girls who lived with their mother in a little cottage. One of the girls had pale golden hair and she was called Snow White. The other had dark hair and rosy cheeks and she was called Rose Red.

The cottage was in the middle of a forest, and every day Snow White and Rose Red would go out to pick flowers for their mother. They knew the forest very well, and no matter how far they wandered, they never got lost.

One cold winter's night, Snow White and Rose Red were cuddled up with their mother by the fire. When suddenly, there was a loud knock at the door.

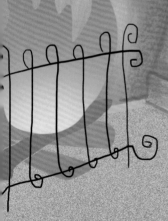

Snow White and Rose Red ran to open the door and saw a big brown bear outside. They screamed and tried to slam the door, but the bear said softly to them, "Please let me in. I am so very cold and hungry."

"Let the poor creature in," said their mother.

Snow White and Rose Red were very scared, but they let the bear come inside. It laid down by the fire and Snow White and Rose Red bought it some food.

"Thank you," said the bear in its deep, growly voice.

They soon realized that the bear was very friendly and meant them no harm. After that, the bear returned to the cottage every day and became friends with Snow White and Rose Red.

They would play hide and seek in the forest and run around in the sunshine having fun. The two girls came to love their new friend. Then, just as spring was beginning, the bear told them that he had to go away.

"I must find my treasure," he said. "It was stolen by and evil dwarf and if I don't get it back by the next full moon, I will stay like this forever!"

The two sisters were puzzled. They wondered what the bear meant, but before they could ask, he had disappeared into the forest.

Some time later, Snow White and Rose Red were out picking flowers when they heard shouting. They followed the noise and found a funny little old man. He was a dwarf whose long beard had got trapped by a falling tree.

"Don't just stand there, help me!" shouted the dwarf rudely. The girls tried to pull him free, but it was no use. Rose Red had an idea. She freed him by cutting the tip of the dwarf's beard off.

Instead of being grateful, the dwarf was furious.

"How dare you cut my beard!" he screamed. He grabbed a sack tied with string and ran away without even saying 'thank you'.

That afternoon, Snow White and Rose Red were walking by a stream when they heard shouting again. Looking down the bank of the stream, they saw that the dwarf had got his beard caught in his fishing rod and a big fish was pulling him into the water.

They grabbed him and pulled hard, but the fish was too big. Again, Rose Red got out her scissors and snipped off more of his beard.

The dwarf was even angrier than before.

"There's hardly any of it left!" he said, angrily.

With that, the dwarf grabbed a second sack tied with string and ran off into the forest.

In the evening, Snow White and Rose Red went to pick some flowers from a pretty meadow. Above them, an enormous eagle was circling. It saw something in the field and swooped down.

Snow White and Rose Red saw that the eagle had grabbed the little dwarf. It was pecking at him and trying to fly off with him.

"Help me!" screamed the dwarf, who was now holding three sacks.

Snow White and Rose Red grabbed the dwarf and pulled him away from the eagle's claws. The eagle flew away, leaving the dwarf's clothes in tatters.

This time, the dwarf was even angrier than before.

"How dare you destroy my clothes, you good-for-nothing fools!" he shouted. "I'm going to teach you a lesson. I'm going to put a horrible curse on both of you and turn you into mice!"

The dwarf raised his arms, but before he could cast his spell, the bear burst out of the forest and bared its teeth. The dwarf ran off into the hills, leaving his three sacks behind.

Snow White and Rose Red opened the sacks. They were full of rubies, emeralds and pearls.

"It's my treasure!" cried the bear.

There was a flash of blinding light and suddenly the bear was gone. In his place, stood a handsome prince.

"I was cursed by that dwarf to roam the forest as a bear, until I could get my treasure back," the prince said. "You have freed me from my curse! We must go to my brother's castle. He thinks I have been dead for many years."

Together, they journeyed to the castle, where the prince's brother was overjoyed to see him. It wasn't long before Snow White and Rose Red married the two brothers and became princesses. They didn't see the wicked dwarf again and both couples lived long, happy lives.

The White Snake

Once upon a time, there was a king who had the knowledge of all things. No one knew how the king knew so much, but every day after dinner, his most trusted servant brought him a secret dish covered with a cloth. Nobody except the king knew what was in the dish.

One day, the servant was so curious that he took the cover off the plate. There, moulded in the shape of a white snake, was a sweet-smelling dish. He couldn't resist eating a tiny piece.

Suddenly, the servant found he could understand the birds outside the window. Eating the magic snake food had given the servant the power to understand what animals were saying!

Later that day, the queen's ring went missing and the servant was accused of stealing it. He ran outside to hide and heard two magpies talking.

"I have a bad tummy ache," said one magpie. "I wish I hadn't accidentally swallowed the queen's ring!"

Quickly, the servant grabbed the magpie and took it to the queen. He gave the magpie a squeeze and it coughed up the missing ring and everyone knew the servant wasn't a thief.

The king rewarded the servant with a gold coin and the servant decided to use it to travel across the land and seek his fortune. As the servant was riding away from the kingdom, he heard some strange voices.

"Help, help!" they said. "We're trapped!"

The voices were coming from a nearby river. The servant got off his horse and found three fish in the river. They were trapped in the reeds and couldn't get out. The servant parted the reeds and let the fish go free.

"Thank you!" said the fish. "We won't forget it."

The servant continued his journey through a forest and heard some more voices.

"We're so hungry!" they cried. He looked around, until he saw three baby doves on the ground. They had fallen out of their nest and couldn't

The servant took pity on the baby birds and shared his lunch with them. Soon, they were strong enough to fly away.

"Thank you!" cried the little doves. "We won't forget it."

After many days of riding, the servant suddenly he heard the sound of many tiny voices.

"Please don't destroy our home," they said.

The servant looked down to see hundreds of tiny ants. "This pile of dirt is our house," they said.

The servant carefully rode his horse around their house.

"Thank you," said the little ants. "We won't forget your kindness!"

Soon, the servant reached the gates of a great castle by the sea. Men from the castle were blowing loud horns and calling out:

"Whoever completes an impossible task will win the king's daughter's hand in marriage!"

When the servant saw the king's daughter and fell in love.

"I must win her hand in marrige," he said. "No matter how hard the task is!"

So the servant came to the castle and told the king he would complete the impossible task. The king took him down to the sea and threw a golden ring far into the water.

"Fetch the ring by tomorrow morning," the king said sternly. "If you do not, my soldiers will throw you into the sea!"

All day, the servant swam in the sea, looking for the ring. It had floated miles away and sunk far too deep for him to reach.

The servant swam and swam until he was worn out. He went to sleep on the sea shore.

"I have failed," he said sadly. "The king's soldiers will throw me in the sea and I will drown!"

Then, at dawn, he heard a splashing sound. It was the three fish he had saved from the reeds. One had the gold ring in its mouth. The servant thanked the fish, and took the ring to the king, but the princess was too proud to marry a servant.

"He must complete another task," she said.

This time, the king's soldiers upset ten huge bags of grain all over the palace gardens.

"Pick up every single grain by morning," said the king. "Or you will never see the princess again!"

The servant tried to pick up the grains, but there were far too many for him, so he fell asleep in despair.

When he woke, he found that the ten sacks were full of grain. Not a single one was missing! His friends the ants had visited him in the night. They had worked hard to put all the grain back in the sacks.

When the princess saw this, she was secretly pleased. But she was too proud to say so.

"Bring me an apple from the Tree of Life at the world's end," she said. "Then I will marry you."

The servant wandered far and wide, but couldn't reach the world's end. As he lay down, ready to give up, he saw three birds flying towards him. It was the baby doves he had fed. They were fully grown and one carried the apple from the Tree of Life in its beak.

Overjoyed, the servant returned to the castle with the apple. This time, even the princess was impressed. There was a celebration and the servant and the princess were married at once.

The Fisherman and His Wife

Once upon a time, a poor fisherman lived with his wife in a tiny shack by the sea. The shack had only one room and its roof was full of holes. Every day, the fisherman rowed out to sea in his tiny, old fishing boat.

"I hope I catch some fish today," he would think to himself. But he never caught enough. The fisherman and his wife often went hungry and cold, until one sunny day when he finally felt a big tug on his line.

"This fish must be huge," he thought, as he reeled it in excitedly. "My wife and I will share such a wonderful meal tonight."

When he finally pulled the fish on board, he saw it looked very different. It was unusually large and covered in yellow and purple stripes.

"I wonder if it's good to eat," said the fisherman.

"Don't eat me!" said the fish. "I'm not very tasty."

"Wow! You can talk?" The fisherman's eyes widened in shock.

"I'm an enchanted fish. I can grant wishes," the fish replied.

"I don't want to eat such a special fish!" said the fisherman. "Don't worry. I'll put you back in the sea."

"Thank you!" said the fish, as the fisherman let him go. "In return, I will grant you a wish."

The fisherman thought about it. "No, no," he said. "I don't want a reward."

"When the fisherman got home that night, he told his wife about the fish.

"You silly man!" said his wife. "Why didn't you take the wish. Tomorrow you will find the fish and ask it for a cottage."

The next day the fisherman rowed back out to sea.

"Little fish! Little fish! Come to me and grant my wish!" the fisherman called. The fish popped out of the water.

"I've changed my mind," said the fisherman. "I wish for a cottage to live in."

"Go home," said the fish. "Your wife is waiting for you in your new cottage!"

Sure enough, when the fisherman got home, he found his tiny shack had been transformed into a pretty little cottage.

"Isn't this wonderful!" said the fisherman to his wife.

For the first few days they were very happy in their cottage, but then the fisherman's wife started to complain.

"Our cottage is too small compared our neighbors'," she said."Go back and ask the magical fish for a mansion."

"My dear, the fish has been very kind," he replied. "We shouldn't ask for more."

"Just do it!" ordered his wife.

The next day, the fisherman rowed out to sea again.

"Little fish! Little fish! Come grant me my wish!" the fisherman called out.

When the fish appeared, the fisherman said that he had changed his mind. "We want a mansion instead."

"Go home," said the fish. "Your wife is waiting for you in your new mansion."

When the fisherman got home, he found the little cottage had turned into a grand house, complete with servants and lots of fine furniture. But the fisherman's wife still wasn't happy.

"The servants are too slow," she said, "and these plates don't go with the wallpaper. Go back to that fish and tell him to change this mansion to a palace. I want to be queen!"

The fisherman was horrified, but he wanted his wife to be happy. He went back out to sea the very next day. This time, the sea was stormy and dark. His little, old boat rocked and bobbed in the waves.

"Little fish! Little fish! Come to me and grant my wish!"

He called out above the howling wind.

"What is it now?" the fish asked.

"My wife wants a palace and she wants to be queen," replied the fisherman, sheepishly.

"Go home," said the fish, "Your wife, the queen is already waiting for you!"

When he got home, the fisherman found his house transformed into a huge palace made of gold.

Soon the fisherman's wife started to complain again. She was tired of sitting on her golden throne.

"I don't like being a queen. Nobody does what I tell them. The other kings and queens probably hate us! What if they invade our country? I would much rather be empress of the whole wide world. Go find that fish and tell him to make me empress."

"But my dear," said the fisherman, "the enchanted fish has already given us so much. What if we make him angry?"

"Who cares?" said his wife. "I want to be empress of the whole world, and I want it now!"

The next day, the fisherman set out in a horrible storm. Thunder rumbled and lightning flashed around him. In a scared voice, the fisherman called out, "Little fish! Little fish! Come to me and grant my wish!"

The fish popped its head out of the water. "What do you want?" he sighed.

The fisherman summoned up all his courage and said, "My wife wants to be empress of the whole world."

"Go home," said the fish, "and see what's waiting for you."

The fisherman rowed back to shore.

When he got home, he found his wife waiting for him, in their tiny old shack!

Queen Bee

Long ago, two brothers set out to find a magic castle. Their younger brother wanted to go too.

"You can come with us," said the older brothers. "But you must do what we say."

On the way, they came to an anthill. The older brothers, who were mean and cruel wanted to push it over.

"No!" cried the kind younger brother.

At a lake, the older brothers wanted to capture the ducks and take them home to eat.

"No!" said the younger brother, "Leave them alone."

Next the older brothers came to a bee hive with a queen bee.

"Let's smoke out the bees and steal their honey," said the older brothers, but again, the younger brother refused to let them.

Soon, the brothers arrived at the castle . Everything was still and quiet. In the stables, the horses had been turned to stone. A stone cat sat on a windowsill and a stone dog slept beneath it.

"It is as if a spell has been cast on it," said the youngest brother.

Just then, the brothers noticed an old man. He was sitting at a stone table in a little room. They called to him and the old man beckoned them to come inside.

"I have three tasks for you," he said. "Whoever completes the tasks will release the castle from the evil spell and marry a beautiful princess."

"Give me a task," said the older brother. "For nothing is too difficult for me."

"Very well," said the old man. "Beneath the moss in the forest are hidden a thousand pearls. Find them and bring them to me before nightfall or you will be turned into stone."

The older brother left immediately. He searched the forest inch by inch, but he only found one pearl and by nightfall he had turned into stone.

"What is my task?" asked the second brother.

"You must find the key in the lake that unlocks the door to the princesses bed chamber," the old man told him.

The second brother left immediately. The water in the lake was cold and deep. He dived into the lake a hundred times, but couldn't find the key and by nightfall, he too, turned into stone.

The youngest brother wondered how he would succeed where his brothers had failed. The old man appeared and asked the youngest brother to bring him the thousand hidden pearls.

As he set off, the youngest brother met the ants he had saved earlier. They had found all the pearls for him.

The old man then set the youngest brother the task of finding the key in the cold, deep lake.

The youngest brother went to the lake.

"We will help you," quacked the ducks who he had saved earlier. In no time at all they had dived into the lake and found the key.

"What shall I do now?" said the youngest brother. Just then the old man appeared.

"You will find three princesses in the castle," he said. "If you can kiss the right one, then the spell will be broken."

The youngest brother set off to the castle to find the princesses.

In the castle the three princesses were asleep.

"Which one must I kiss?" asked the youngest brother.

"The one who has eaten honey," said a little voice. It was the queen Bee from the hive he had saved.

The queen bee flew to the middle princess and buzzed loudly.

"This is the one," she said.

The youngest brother kissed the princess and the spell was broken and everything came back to life.

The youngest brother fell in love with the princess and they married soon after. His brothers were never cruel or mean again and every time they saw a queen bee, they smiled.

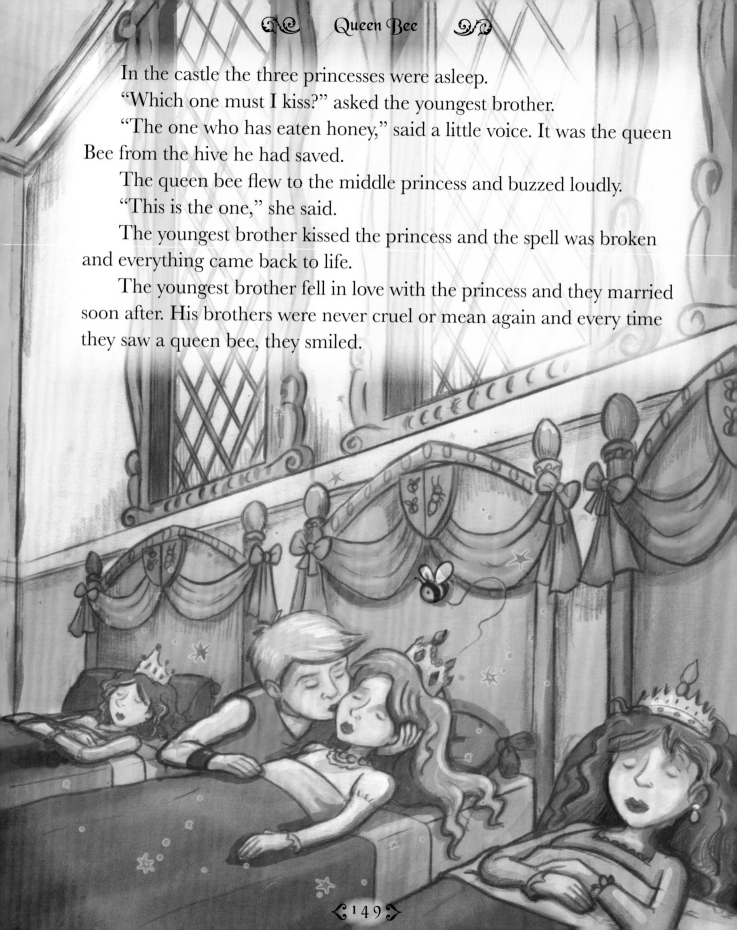

Jorinda and Joringel

Once there was a wicked witch who could disguise herself as an owl. The witch did not like pretty girls and if any came near her castle, she would change them into songbirds and put them in cages.

As it happened, a beautiful young girl called Jorinda lived close to the witch and one day, she went for a picnic there with her sweetheart, Joringel. The pair were so happy to be together they took no notice of where they were going.

Soon, they found themselves at the witch's castle. High on a ledge, a large owl hooted.

"To-whit, to-whoo!"

The owl flew down and circled round Jorinda and Joringel three times. Suddenly, they couldn't move or speak.

As quick as a flash the owl changed into the cruel witch.

"Now I have you," she cried, pointing a bony finger at Jorinda.

In a flash of light, Jorinda was turned into a nightingale. The witch grabbed the bird, shut it in a cage and ran into the castle.

Joringel was heartbroken. He was powerless against the witch. There was nothing he could do to rescue Jorinda, so he made his way sadly back home.

That night, Joringel dreamed about a beautiful red flower that could free everything from the witch's spell. It grew in a strange and barren land that was far away.

"I must find the flower," said Joringel , waking up and he set off without delay.

Joringel walked through valleys and over mountains, until his legs ached and his shoes were torn. He searched day and night without rest.

After many days, he found what he was looking for. Hidden in a crack in a rock was the bright red flower and in its centre was a dew drop as big as a pearl.

Joringel made his way back to the castle. As he approached, he took out the red flower and held it in front of him. The castle gates sprung open and he heard the sound of birdsong. Joringel followed the sound to the room with all the bird cages.

"Which one is Jorinda?" he said, looking round at all the bird cages.

Just then he caught sight of the witch. She was sneaking away, carrying one of the cages.

"Stop!" cried Joringel.

The witch turned to face him.

"Stay away," she hissed and fired a spell from her magic wand.

Joringel held the red flower in front of him and the spell exploded in a thousand sparkles that flashed and disappeared.

Joringel was unharmed and the witch shrieked with rage.

"You will never have her," screamed the witch, holding up the cage with Jorinda inside. "She will die first."

As quick as a flash, Joringel leant forward and touched the witch with the bright red flower. She let out a terrible wailing scream, dropped the cage and crumpled to the ground in a heap of ash.

Joringel caught the cage as it fell. The door opened and the little nightingale flew out. Joringel touched it with the flower and the spell was broken. In front of him was his sweetheart, Jorinda. He knelt in front of her.

"Will you marry me ? he asked.

"Yes, I will," said Jorinda, kissing him," but first we must remove the spell from the other birds."

One by one, the birds were turned back into pretty girls. They thanked Jorinda and Joringel with tears of joy.

Hand in hand Jorinda and Joringel returned to their village where they lived a long and happy life.

Sweet Porridge

Once upon a time, a little girl lived alone with her mother. They were very poor and quite often didn't have enough to eat. One day the little girl said to her mother. "I am so hungry. Is there some bread we could eat for breakfast?"

The mother put her arms round the little girl, for she loved her very much.

"Dear child," she said. "We have nothing to eat today. The cupboard is bare. Go into the woods and look for some nuts and berries."

"Of course I will," said the little girl and she kissed her mother and set off. She hadn't gone far when she saw an old lady.

"What are you looking for child," asked the old lady.

"Some nuts and berries," said the little girl. "My mother and I have nothing to eat."

The old lady felt sorry for the little girl.

"This will help you," she said and she gave her a very special pot. "Cook, little pot, cook," ordered the old lady and the little pot cooked some good sweet porridge.

Then the old lady said, "Stop, little pot, stop," and the little pot stopped cooking. "You will never be hungry again," she told the girl.

The little girl thanked the old lady and ran home.

The girl showed the pot to her mother.

"What is that?' her mother asked.

"It's a magic pot," the little girl told her, putting the pot on the table.

"Cook, little pot, cook," she said to the pot, and the pot cooked enough sweet porridge for them both.

"Stop, little pot, stop," said the girl, and the pot stopped cooking.

The mother was amazed.

"That is wonderful," she said to her daughter. "You have done well." She put her arms round the little girl and hugged her.

That night the mother and the little girl ate a good meal and went to bed feeling full and happy.

The next day, the little girl had to visit her aunt.
"I will be back tomorrow," she said to her mother when she left.

That evening the mother was hungry.

"I'll ask the pot to cook me some porridge," she thought. "Cook, little pot, cook," ordered the mother, and the little pot cooked her some porridge.

"Stop," said the mother when there was enough, but the pot didn't stop. The mother had forgotten the magic words and the pot went on cooking. Soon, porridge filled the house and flowed out of the door, down the street.

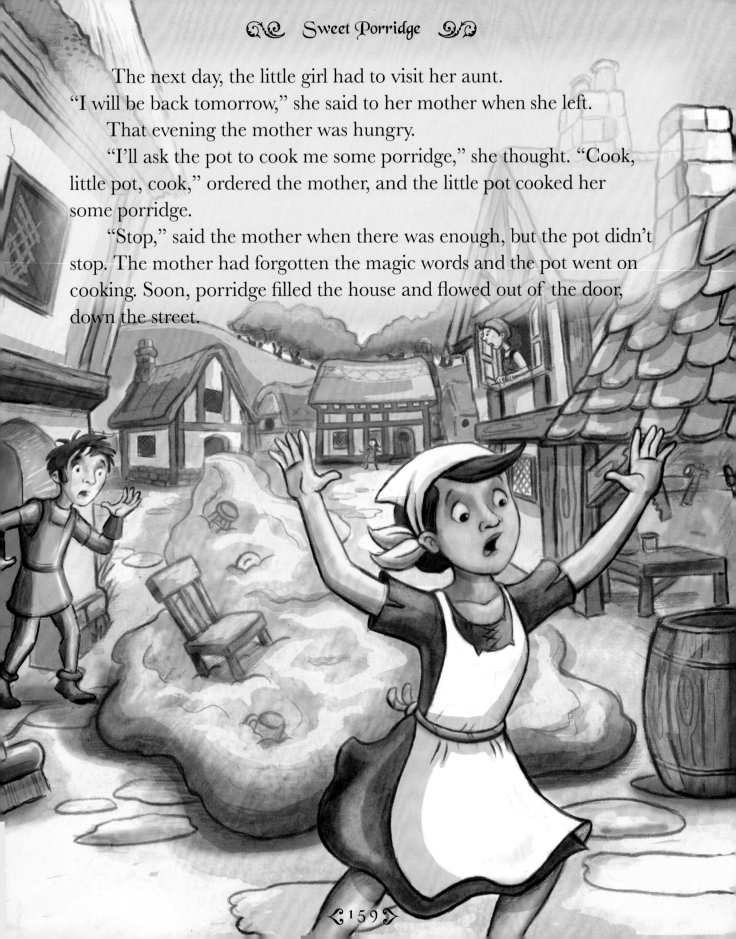

It wasn't long before nearly the whole town was full of porridge.
"What will we do?" asked the townspeople.

Just then, the little girl came back. "Stop, little pot, stop!" she cried and suddenly the pot stopped.

"There's only one thing you can do," replied the girl. "You must eat your way back into your houses."

So, everyone got bowls and pots of honey and start to eat. They all had a wonderful time gobbling up the sweet porridge and after that, no one ever went hungry again.